For Snowball, Albus, and Squeak

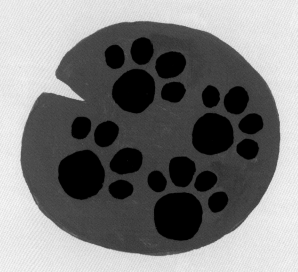

First American edition 2006, published by Houghton Mifflin Company

Originally published in the United Kingdom by Egmont Books Limited

www.houghtonmifflinbooks.com

ISBN-13: 978-0618-47300-7

Manufactured in Singapore
10 9 8 7 6 5 4 3 2

Do Lions Live on Lily Pads?

melanie walsh

Is this the nest of a goat?

No, it belongs to a bird.

Do crocodiles live in shells?

No, but
snails do.

Is this the burrow
of a giraffe?

Do parakeets live in bowls?

No, but fish do.

Do guinea pigs live in webs?

No, but spiders do.

Do fleas live in fur?

Yes! Scratch, scratch!